THE ADVENTURES OF

HARRY STEVENSON

THE ADVENTURES OF
HARRY STEVENSON

SIMON & SCHUSTER

**To Uncle Pete. Thanks for
giving Mum those guinea pigs
all those years ago!**

First published in Great Britain in 2019
by Simon & Schuster UK Ltd,
A CBS COMPANY.

1 3 5 7 9 10 8 6 4 2

Simon & Schuster UK Ltd
1st Floor, 222 Gray's Inn Road, London WC1X 8HB

www.simonandschuster.co.uk
www.simonandschuster.com.au
www.simonandschuster.co.in

Simon & Schuster Australia, Sydney
Simon & Schuster India, New Delhi

A CIP catalogue record for this book is available from the British Library.

PB ISBN 978-1-4711-7023-2
EBook ISBN 978-1-4711-7024-9

Printed in China

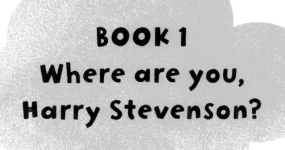

BOOK 1
Where are you, Harry Stevenson?

CHAPTER 1

Pleased to meet you, Harry Stevenson

It seemed just like every other morning. The sun peeped into the cage that belonged to Harry Stevenson, a plump and very ordinary-looking guinea pig. As usual, Harry was snoring loudly and dreaming about food. Snoozing and dreaming about food was how Harry Stevenson spent most of his time. That was when he wasn't *eating* food, of course, or reading the newspaper that lined his cage.

A sparkly ray of sunshine tickled Harry Stevenson's whiskers, but Harry didn't stir. He was snuggled up inside a cosy pile of hay. Harry always enjoyed a lie-in in the morning. He liked one in the afternoon too.

He was also very fond of lie-ins during the evening, between his after-dinner nap and bedtime.

The hay shook gently as Harry Stevenson snored in his nest. Every now and again, he would smack his lips as he dreamed about carrots and broccoli, nuggets and hay.

Yes, everything seemed normal that morning – but it wouldn't stay like that. Harry didn't know it yet, but he was about to have a **VERY** unusual day.

GROOOOOWWWWWLLLLLL!!!

Harry Stevenson woke up with a jump.

Yikes! What was that horrible loud noise? An angry dog? An escaped tiger? A *dragon*? Harry looked around in panic but there weren't any dogs, lions or dragons. It was just his empty tummy rumbling. It did that a lot.

Harry hurried over to his food bowl. A few tasty nuggets would start the day off nicely. A lot of tasty nuggets would start it off even better. Then he could settle down to read the newspaper: perhaps there'd be some gossip pages lining the cage today, or the football reports. Harry loved to read about his favourite team, Sparky FC.

But when Harry reached the bowl he got a nasty surprise. He blinked a few times –

were his eyes working properly? For there in front of him was a horrible sight . . . **AN EMPTY BOWL!**

Harry gulped. This was bad! Where had all his food gone? He'd only eaten a little bit of dinner. His midnight feast had been very small – not really a feast at all. As for his night-snack, well, that had just been a couple of carrots. Ah! It must have been that emergency picnic at 5am.

No matter. Harry knew exactly what to do. Like a small, furry and incredibly loud fire alarm, he lifted his head and sounded the emergency klaxon . . .

'WHEEEEEEKKKKKKKKKKKKKKK!!!!!!
WHEEEEEEKKKKKKKKKKKKKKK!!!!!!
WHEEEEEEKKKKKKKKKKKKKKK!!!!!!'

It never failed! Harry heard footsteps and in came Billy.

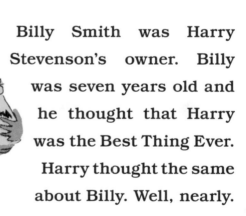

Billy Smith was Harry Stevenson's owner. Billy was seven years old and he thought that Harry was the Best Thing Ever. Harry thought the same about Billy. Well, nearly.

If Harry had to choose between Billy and a pile of carrots and spinach, he would have to think very hard before choosing Billy. He *was* a guinea pig after all.

Harry's cage rested on a table in the corner of Billy's room. Once Billy had reached inside the cage to refill the bowl, Harry Stevenson guzzled nuggets like he hadn't eaten for days.

'Eat up, Harry,' said Billy. 'It's a big day today – we're moving house!'

Harry Stevenson almost choked on his nuggets. Moving house? How would the Smiths manage to move a whole house? Billy was only small. Mr and Mrs Smith were grown-ups, but surely even they weren't strong enough to pick up a house and move it?

What if they dropped the house, with Harry inside? Even worse – what if the nuggets, and the carrots, and the spinach somehow *fell out* when the house was moving?

This needed thinking about. But thinking was hungry work – so Harry decided to eat first and worry later. After he'd had a sleep, of course.

CHAPTER 2

What's going on, Harry Stevenson?

But Harry Stevenson never got that sleep because Billy wanted to talk. Billy reached into the cage and gently scooped up Harry – or at least as much of Harry as a seven-year-old could hold. Harry's tummy draped over the sides of Billy's hands like a warm, fluffy cushion, or a lovely soft cake that has risen over the side of the tin. Harry stifled an indignant squeak. He was a polite animal and didn't want to hurt Billy's feelings. Billy lay down on the bed and sighed, placing Harry Stevenson on his chest. Boy and guinea pig faced each other: nose to nose, freckle to whisker.

'We're going to live in a new flat, Harry,' said Billy as he stroked Harry's fur. 'This is our last morning here.'

Harry Stevenson looked deep into Billy's eyes. Although Harry could never be described as a clever animal, there was one subject in which he was a world-class expert: Billy. And right now Harry could sense something strange. Billy was feeling lots of different things, all at the same time. He was happy and sad, scared and excited. It was very odd!

Harry wondered why Billy felt like that. But Harry couldn't ask, so he did the next best thing, which was to nuzzle Billy's chin with his furry nose. Then he tickled Billy's cheeks with his waggly whiskers. Billy giggled. Ah, that was better!

'You're the best, Harry!' Billy said. 'I like it here. I don't want to move. But the new flat is bigger, I guess, and it's got a garden too. You can run around outside, Harry.'

Harry Stevenson didn't like the sound of *outside*. As far as Harry was concerned, the world ended at the door of the flat. All he knew was Billy's bedroom (where Harry ate, slept and read the paper) and a place called 'the living room', where the Smiths, well, lived. But mostly they watched TV and ate biscuits there. 'Outside' was like Outer Space to Harry – it was something that went on at a safe distance, thank you very much.

Harry thought that 'Outside' should just carry on going about its business while he minded his own in the cage.

And outside was *dangerous*. It was where the predators lived! Harry had watched plenty of nature programmes with Billy. He'd seen enough to know that outside was no picnic if you were small, furry and plump. Instead, you *were* the picnic. Outside was bristling with hungry hawks, starving snakes and famished foxes just waiting to pounce. Harry crouched down and shook his whiskers in fear. No, he didn't want to go outside.

'Don't worry, Harry,' said Billy, who could sense that his friend was unhappy. 'I'll look after you.'

Safe in Billy's arms, Harry felt a bit better. He'd stay there all day if he could.

Over the next few hours Harry watched as the world he knew was packed up and put into boxes. Harry didn't like this at all. If guinea pigs could scowl, Harry Stevenson would have looked very grumpy indeed. He burrowed deep into his pile of hay and peeped out, with only his nose and whiskers showing. Even his whiskers looked cross.

First Mr and Mrs Smith helped Billy take down his posters of Sparky FC from the walls. Harry chuntered his disapproval from the hay. He saw the books that Billy had read him being packed away, and his favourite soft blanket from Billy's bed folded up into a suitcase.

Every now and again, Mr and Mrs Smith would hold up a toy or a book and ask the same question: 'Do you still want this, Billy?' They always got the same answer. Each time, Billy folded his arms and nodded his head.

Harry knew why – it was bad enough having to move without being asked to get rid of special things! Mr and Mrs Smith would sigh and place the books and toys in an ever-growing pile of boxes.

Once Billy's room was packed up, the

Smiths moved on to the other rooms. Harry watched through Billy's bedroom door as they stacked all the furniture up on its end. It was hard work and everyone got very cross. Mr Smith dropped a china fox that Mrs Smith was very fond of and it broke.

Mrs Smith **NEVER** normally shouted, but she did just then! Harry trembled in his hay.

Soon there was nothing left but a big pile of boxes and a jumble of furniture stacked up in the middle of every room. Even the curtains were taken down. The windows looked bigger without them and there were faded marks on the wall where Billy's posters had been. Now the flat didn't feel like a home – it was a strange, unfamiliar space.

Harry thought of all the good times he'd had there: watching Sparky FC win the Cup Final on TV; that time he'd discovered a forgotten bit of carrot behind a cushion on the sofa; and every single day keeping an eye on Billy from his cosy nest.

That was all over now. It was all *very* odd.

CHAPTER 3

Don't panic,
Harry Stevenson

Harry Stevenson had nodded off. The noise of footsteps woke him up and he sleepily looked around. Billy's room was nearly empty. The boxes of toys and books and the upturned furniture had gone. Only Harry's cage remained.

Through the window Harry could see

Mr Smith's van. It had once been white and smart, but it was hard to tell that now. Harry always knew when Mr Smith got home from work because the van backfired with a noise that sent him leaping into the air with fright. Funnily enough, Harry didn't like the van very much.

Mr and Mrs Smith were carrying boxes out of the flat and putting them in the back of the van. They didn't seem so cross now. Well, that was something good at least.

The footsteps got nearer – Billy was coming. Aha, this could be promising! Was it snack time? Harry **wheeked** hopefully. But instead of food Billy was carrying a big bag of hay.

'It's nearly time to go, Harry,' he said. 'We need to fill your cage up so you feel safe on the journey.' And he stuffed the cage completely full of hay. Harry snuggled deep inside and curled up in the middle. He decided to stay there, hidden and safe, until this whole 'journey' thing was over.

But then poor Harry got another shock. His cage was lifted high into the air. And, even worse, it was moving! **YIKES!** Harry closed his eyes tightly and thought of comforting things like bowls of nuggets, or Sparky FC beating

their rivals 25–0, but it was no use. Even thoughts of Billy couldn't calm him down. When would this horrible day end?

'Just pop him down here for a bit,' he heard Mrs Smith say. 'Let's do that last room.'

Harry stirred in the hay. Something felt different. Was it the light, the temperature or the smell? Well, yes – it was all of those things!

Very cautiously, Harry Stevenson stuck the tip of his nose out of the hay. He smelled the air: **Sniff, Sniff, Sniff.** Ooh! It was different, full of new scents. Harry gave a little jump of excitement. Guinea pigs do this when they're happy – it's called 'popcorning' because they suddenly leap into the air like a piece of corn bursting in a pan!

Harry poked his nose out a little more. He twitched his whiskers. *Hmmm* – it was a bit cold compared to the warmth of Billy's room. Maybe the heating had been turned off in the flat?

Harry's nose and whiskers had done their job – now it was time to use his eyes. He poked his face further out of the hay. He looked once, looked twice – and realized the dreadful truth!

HARRY STEVENSON WAS OUTSIDE.

THE END

CHAPTER 4

Is it the end, Harry Stevenson?

Well, it might not **REALLY** have been the end for Harry Stevenson – but it definitely felt like it!

He was outside. Outside: that fearsome place! Any moment now, Harry Stevenson was going to be gobbled up by something ferocious and hungry, just like in those nature programmes he'd seen with Billy. Harry cowered in the hay, covering his eyes with shaking paws. He braced himself for the talons and fangs to come.

It was only a matter of time now. The end was nigh! He'd had a good life – he couldn't complain (although perhaps there could have been a *bit* more food). But now he WAS food! Maybe it would be quick – one chew and a gulp. Actually, Harry didn't want to think about that . . .

He would just have to close his eyes and wait.

So Harry waited

and waited

and waited.

But no claws or talons came. Perhaps the hawks, snakes and foxes were polishing off some other unfortunate creature for starters? Yes, that would be it. Licking their chops and getting ready for the main course: Harry.

So he waited some more.

After a while it got a bit boring. Perhaps the end wasn't nigh JUST yet after all. Harry stopped quivering and calmed down. Soon he started to feel better. But, as the fear went away, something else filled its place – hunger!

Harry Stevenson popped his head out of the hay for a second and took a quick peep up at the sky.

There were no hawks hovering above – *good!* Harry looked again. No prowling foxes or lurking snakes – *phew!*

Now Harry could look around properly. He saw that his cage was perched on a wall to the side of the Smiths' flat. It was a very long wall, running all the way down the street. In fact, it went off further than Harry's eyes could see, far away into the distance. But Harry wasn't interested in the end of the wall. Something much nearer had grabbed his attention.

Next to the wall was a bank and on the bank were big clumps of what Harry recognized as dandelion plants. Harry knew ALL about dandelions. Billy had sometimes picked them from this very bank and brought them in for Harry.

Harry loved dandelions. He really, really did. But, to reach these ones, Harry would have to leave his cage. That would be dangerous and Harry would never do anything so silly . . .

. . . would he?

CHAPTER 5

Don't do it,
Harry Stevenson!

The dandelions growing on the bank had fresh green leaves. Some were big, some were small, but every single leaf looked delicious. They were so new and delicate that the sun shone through them and a soft green light gleamed from the plants. Fluffy seed heads and vivid yellow flowers nodded in the breeze. Harry Stevenson stared in wonder. And then he imagined just how good those dandelions would taste.

Harry longed to leave the cage, but he knew that he shouldn't. Billy trusted him and Harry couldn't let him down. So he took one last look at the dandelions and turned back into the hay. The sports pages of the newspaper were lining the cage. He settled down to read the latest on Sparky FC, who had won their last three games. The Sparkies were doing well, thought Harry – Billy would be pleased.

Just then, a gust of breeze wafted into the hay. Harry Stevenson sniffed the air: dandelions! Harry's whiskers trembled –

but he took a deep breath and tried to focus on Sparky FC's midfield strategy.

The scent grew stronger and even lovelier. Harry's mouth watered. The words on the newspaper danced before his eyes. Some of the letters even seemed to turn into dandelion seeds and floated away from the page. Harry forced himself to focus and the words became clear again.

But then another breath of wind filled the whole cage with the wonderful perfume of dandelions. It was the smell of spring, of sunshine, of tasty green leaves. Harry's tummy gave a mighty rumble.

Harry Stevenson could ignore his trembly whiskers or watery mouth, but a rumbly belly was too much. He just *had* to taste those dandelions! In desperation, Harry shut his eyes and tried squeaking to ten. But, by the time he'd got to four squeaks, his paws seemed to be moving all by themselves. By five squeaks he was stepping towards the cage door. By six he was pushing the door open with his nose and by seven he had stepped out of the cage!

Never mind squeaking to ten – Harry didn't even get to seven and a half! Before he knew it, he'd dived right into the middle of the dandelions and was scoffing a huge mouthful of leaves.

Mmm, those dandelions really were delicious! Harry Stevenson ate

and ate

and ate.

Hidden within the dandelion patch, Harry Stevenson was so busy stuffing himself that he didn't hear the Smith family walk back down the path. He didn't hear them lift the cage off the wall and he didn't hear them load it into the van.

It was only when the van doors slammed shut that Harry looked up. He poked his head out of the dandelions to see what was going on. There was the van – but where were the Smiths? Harry looked at the van again and saw that everyone was inside. He looked closer. That was odd – Mr Smith was starting the engine and Billy was looking out of the window. He seemed to be waving at the flat. Why was he doing that?

And then, with a noisy backfire and a cheery **toot toot** of the horn, the van drove off down the road.

All at once Harry Stevenson understood. Nobody had spotted that Harry wasn't in his cage! The door had swung shut after he'd opened it and there was too much hay to see inside. Nobody had noticed Harry in the dandelions either. Well, why would they?

He was supposed to be minding his own business in the hay, not sneaking around outside, scoffing dandelions.

No, the Smiths had driven away in their van, completely unaware that one of the family was missing.

Harry Stevenson had been left behind!!!

CHAPTER 6

Run,
Harry Stevenson!

Harry Stevenson could move fast when he wanted to – which wasn't often, as you will have gathered by now. But occasionally, and especially where food was involved, he could scamper like a streak of lightning – if lightning could be fluffy, tubby and ginger.

So Harry streaked off now: like fluffy,

tubby, ginger lightning. He had to catch up with Billy! His friend NEEDED him, especially on a difficult day like this. How would Billy cope with the move without Harry to help him? True, earlier in the day Billy had said he'd look after Harry – but Harry looked after Billy too!

Harry sped along the wall as he chased the van down the street. His belly went **BUMPETY BUMP** against the top of the wall every now and again, but he kept going. It was hard work! Harry could still

see the van though. It was at the end of the street, waiting to turn on to the main road. Luckily, there was a lot of traffic. Mr Smith was having to wait a long time.

Harry raced along in a blur of ginger fur. Occasionally, he gave a little **SQUEAK** of panic. He had to catch up with the van and somehow get back into his cage. He didn't know how and there was no time to think of a plan; he just had to keep that van in his sights. How cosy and friendly it looked now, despite its dirty doors. Harry would have

given anything to be safely inside with Billy.

Harry ran as fast as he could, desperate to catch up with his friend. He ran as if his life depended on it. Which, as Harry realized with horror, it actually *did*! For all of a sudden he heard footsteps behind him. They were soft, light and fast and were getting closer and closer. Something was chasing him!

Harry looked behind and gave a squeal of terror. On his tail was a TIGER! A huge, hungry tiger with fierce yellow eyes and big scary teeth!

YIKES! thought Harry. This was just like the wildlife programmes. Harry was **PREY!!!**

'Come back, little one,' hissed the tiger as it ran. 'Come back and play.'

The tiger wasn't really a tiger, of course – it was just a big old pussycat from across the street. The 'tiger' even had a name – Mr Snuggles. Harry Stevenson had never seen a cat before. He'd seen plenty of tigers on TV though – so you can understand why he was mistaken. And Mr Snuggles WAS looking quite tigerish as he chased poor Harry.

Harry looked ahead desperately. The van was still there, waiting

at the end of the road. If Harry could just reach it before it turned, he could somehow attract the Smiths' attention. Maybe he could jump up and down? Maybe he could give his loudest **WHEEK?** Something, anything would do!

He had to make it! Not long to go now: five metres, four metres. The tiger was getting closer. Harry could hear the click of its claws on the wall and feel its hot breath on his fur.

Three metres, two metres: nearly there! The tiger tried to biff Harry with its paws, but he leaped ahead in the nick of time. Just one last burst and he'd reach the van.

Surely the Smiths would notice him? They *had* to see him!

One metre to go! The end of the wall zoomed up towards Harry. But, just as Harry reached it, lots of things happened all at once and not one of them was good.

The traffic on the main road cleared and the Smiths' van finally turned out of the street.

Mr Snuggles pounced, yowling in deadly triumph and with his terrible claws outstretched . . .

And Harry Stevenson did the only thing he could think of, which was to close his eyes and take a flying LEAP off the wall.

UP, UP, UP into the air went that fat little guinea pig, with Mr Snuggles hissing and spitting behind.

'WWHHHHEEEEEEEEEE EEEEEEEEKKKKKKKKK!!!!' squealed Harry Stevenson. Special moments of his life flashed before his eyes: snuggling up to Billy, snoozing in the hay, scoffing a whole bag of tasty spinach. Poor Harry Stevenson! There was no escape now.

CHAPTER 7

Follow that van,
Harry Stevenson

Harry Stevenson flew through the air like a ginger comet, squealing with terror . . . and landed with a **SPLAT** on something squidgy.

'OOOOF!' said Harry Stevenson, winded by his landing. He crouched down flat and lay very still, his little heart beating fast. **PUFF, PUFF, PUFF,** he panted, catching his breath after such a fright (not to mention the sprint along the wall).

Harry looked around. Where was he? He seemed to be in some kind of cage – but it was very different from his cage at home. The sides were made of wood, not metal, and there was no roof, only the sky above. Strangely, the sky seemed to be moving. And – even odder – he was sharing the cage with five grapefruits, a loaf of bread and a newspaper. One of the grapefruits must have been a bit rotten because it had burst when Harry landed on it. Now he was covered in soggy bits of fruit. Harry tried to nibble a piece and quickly spat it out again. *Ugh!* It was very sour.

Harry realized that to see out of the cage he would have to climb up on to the grapefruits. This was quite difficult as not only were they round and slippy but they kept rolling about. Every time Harry got to the top, they seemed to move, sending him scrabbling to the bottom again. It took a few attempts for Harry climb up. He cautiously poked his head over the top of the cage and looked around.

Oh dear.

Harry wasn't in a cage – he'd landed in a wicker basket. Not just any old basket though – it was a special one attached to the back of a bicycle. The bicycle appeared to be moving quite fast. Harry looked at the

cyclist, but he could only see the person's back. Then he turned round to look behind him. There was Mr Snuggles, sitting on the end of the wall and looking extremely cross. The cat's eyes flashed with hatred and he

bared his teeth at Harry, who ducked back down in fear.

After a while, Harry felt brave enough to look ahead again. The basket was wide and stuck out over either side of the back wheel. That meant that Harry could see beyond the cyclist, on to the road ahead. He realized with joy that the bike was headed in the same direction as the van – which wasn't too far in front. Harry even got a glimpse of Billy in the back seat!

The traffic stopped and started, and the cyclist puffed along as the road passed a park. There was a playground with swings and slides, and a large playing field with goalposts set up. Harry realized that this must be the place where Billy played football. He was always talking about meeting his friends for a kick-about.

Normally, Harry would have enjoyed discovering more about Billy's life outside the flat. But not like this: balancing on grapefruits, hiding in a stranger's wicker basket in pursuit of a scruffy old van and facing the very real danger of never seeing Billy again.

Up ahead, Harry saw that the van was turning on to a road that cut across the park. Would the cyclist follow?

But just then, at the worst possible moment, Harry noticed that the cyclist was waving to a lady in a pink coat who was walking along the side of the park. And now the bike was slowing down and they were stopping to chat!

Not now, please! thought Harry in dismay.

Harry had to act and fast. Suddenly, he spotted a big, shaggy-looking dog ambling along. It was getting closer to the bike, having a really good sniff of everything it passed. Soon it was by the bicycle and started to sniff the wheels.

Harry Stevenson looked at the van speeding away and he looked at the dog. Then he looked at the van again . . . and back at the dog. Harry didn't know a lot about dogs, but this one seemed to have quite big teeth. It would almost certainly count as a predator. Harry gulped. He knew exactly what he had to do, but he didn't want to do it. That dog was bad news, but if Harry wanted to see Billy again there was no other option.

So, for the second time that day, Harry Stevenson LEAPED up into the air – and landed on the back of the dog with the big teeth.

CHAPTER 8

Hold on,
Harry Stevenson!

The dog barked in surprise. He tried to turn his head round to see what had landed on his back. But Harry Stevenson had scrambled up on to the dog's neck. So, whenever the dog moved his head, Harry moved too and stayed just out of sight. The dog turned round and round in circles, frantically trying to see behind his head. It looked like he was chasing his tail.

The dog circled faster and faster and Harry Stevenson began to feel dizzy. Then he started to wobble. He was going to fall off! Harry's paws scrabbled in the shaggy dog fur, but it was no use. Harry couldn't hold on much longer. He was starting to slip!

Despite his big teeth, the dog was a kind and lovely animal. He was a good boy, who 'sat' when he was told to. So he really didn't deserve what happened next. It was something that spoiled his 'walkies' in the park for quite some time. You see, as Harry Stevenson felt himself falling, he opened his mouth wide and bit down hard on the dog's fur.

Like all guinea pigs, Harry always took great care of his teeth and would never risk damaging them, but desperate times call for desperate measures and Harry needed to try anything to hold on. He must have bitten harder than he meant to though, for the dog yelped in pain and started to run like the clappers!

'MACK!' called the lady in the pink coat as the dog raced off. But her pet kept running.

Mouth full of fur, Harry held on grimly. He bounced up and down like a rodeo rider as Mack belted across the park, howling with fear of the unknown thing on his back. He didn't notice the small group of people flying kites. **SLAM!!!** Mack and Harry ran straight into the group and ended up with kites and streamers dragging behind them as they went.

Amazingly, the kite strings didn't slow Mack down – but they tripped up everyone in their path and so alerted every single dog nearby. They could all see that something MUCH more exciting than fetching sticks was going on.

Ooh, a chase! thought the dogs happily. They followed in hot pursuit, barking madly and waving their tails with glee.

With Mack leading the way, the whole pack streaked across a rugby pitch, where the players had just started a scrum. Harry Stevenson closed his eyes and ducked down flat as Mack ran right through the middle of the scrum and out again. The dogs behind tried to follow, but there were too many of them to get through.

BOOM!! A yapping, shaggy whirlwind of terriers, bloodhounds, spaniels and Labradors collided with the rugby players. There was an angry muddle of yelping and cursing and growling and shouting. Then

the dogs picked themselves up and charged
on. They left a pile of big burly rugby players
collapsed in a heap, tangled up in kite string
and scratching their heads in confusion.

As Mack thundered on, Harry Stevenson risked another look ahead. He tried to spot the van. There it was! But oh no, what was this? *Yikes!* A picnic was coming up fast!

Harry could hear happy laughs and chatter, but that suddenly changed to shouts. In an instant, the baying pack of dogs had clattered through the picnic, spilling drinks and sending food flying. Cake, biscuits, sandwiches and sausage rolls flew through the air to a soundtrack of crying children. All the other dogs stopped chasing Harry to gobble up the food.

But Harry didn't notice any of these things (well, apart from a delicious blob of strawberry jelly that had landed on Mack). He focused on the van ahead. Mack was catching it up. They were nearly there!

Just as Harry thought everything would be all right, something happened to prove him wrong. Mack started to slow down. Harry tried giving him a nip, but the dog no longer seemed to notice. Instead, Mack skidded to a halt and eagerly sniffed the air. With a sinking feeling, Harry spotted a delivery driver parking his moped and dropping off some boxes to a group of teenagers sitting on a bench. As they opened the boxes, Harry saw the pizzas inside. Oh dear! Billy loved pizza – and it looked like Mack did too.

As Mack trotted hungrily over to the teenagers, Harry saw the Smiths' van speed up and drive away. He looked around. There were no traffic jams to slow the van, no bicycles or dogs to ride this time. He'd never run fast enough to catch up on his own.

The van turned a corner and disappeared from view. This was it. Harry Stevenson was on his own!

CHAPTER 9

Where have you gone, Harry Stevenson?

Things weren't going too well for the rest of the Smith family either.

At first, everything had seemed fine. The van whizzed out of the park and sped on to another part of the city. It pulled up outside a modern, low block of flats – this was the Smiths' new home. Mr and Mrs Smith led

Billy up the path, past a rose bush and some cheery-looking garden gnomes. Billy eyed them grumpily. He couldn't see what there was to be jolly about.

'Chin up, Billy,' said Mr Smith. 'Come and look around, then show Harry your new room. He'll love it – and you will too!'

Proudly, Mr Smith unlocked the door of the new flat and together the family went inside. The flat was warm and bright with sunlight. It smelled of fresh paint. As the Smiths looked around, Billy had to admit that it really would make a very nice place to live. Perfect, in fact.

Or so it seemed.

The new flat was certainly bigger and yes, it had a lovely garden too. But, as soon as the Smiths started to unpack the van, they realized their new home was missing something **VERY IMPORTANT INDEED.**

A plump, furry, squeaky something . . .

'Harry?' said Billy with his hands in the cage, feeling in the hay for his friend.

But the hay was cold and the cage was empty.

'HARRY!!!!' cried Billy.

'I just can't understand it,' said Mr Smith, scratching his head. 'Harry must still be in the van somewhere. Let's go and look.'

Mrs Smith gathered up Billy in a huge hug. 'Harry can't have gone far – he's much too lazy for that.'

'Come on,' said Mr Smith, 'let's check that van.'

Soon they were all poking around in the back of the van. Or at least they were trying to. It was getting dark by now so it was almost impossible to see. Mr Smith tripped over a garden gnome and used a very bad word. No one could find the torches, of course. They were still packed up in a box in the van. Mrs Smith decided to knock next door and see if they could borrow one.

A friendly-looking lady came to the door, with a girl of Billy's age hiding behind her. Billy was sure he'd seen the lady somewhere before, but he couldn't work out where. After a quick chat, the Smiths learned that she was called Mrs Matthews and her daughter's name was Maya. They also found out that

while Mrs Matthews was chatty and kind, Maya didn't say much at all. She seemed a **VERY** quiet sort of girl.

Mrs Matthews bustled about trying to find a torch. Then everyone climbed into the back of the van and peered into the boxes. They found all sorts of things, including the missing torches, and Mr Smith's long-lost favourite shirt, which was orange and flowery and had mysteriously disappeared several years ago. Mrs Smith went a bit pink when *that* turned up, for some reason. But there was no sign of Harry, not even a squeak.

Soon there was nothing more to be done. Every box had been searched; every corner of the van had been checked, but Harry Stevenson was nowhere to be found. Everyone felt very sad. It had been a long and tiring day.

Mr and Mrs Smith thanked Mrs Matthews. Then they put their arms round Billy and walked with him up the path. Billy said nothing at all. Even when Mr Smith ordered takeaway pizzas to cheer everyone up, Billy stayed silent. He loved his guinea pig and he would miss him so much. Things would never be the same again.

CHAPTER 10

Extra pepper on that, Harry Stevenson?

What a sad scene it was, that first unhappy evening in the Smiths' new flat. No one felt like doing much, so the family sat on the floor, surrounded by wrapped-up furniture and boxes. Mr and Mrs Smith tried their best to cheer Billy up, but they were feeling very glum themselves.

Then the doorbell rang. It was the first time they'd heard it – it played a silly tune. Suddenly, everyone thought of how much they missed the old flat, with its plain *ding-dongy* doorbell, and with Harry fast asleep in his cage.

The doorbell rang again.

'That'll be the takeaway,' said Mrs Smith. 'Come on, Billy!'

'I don't feel hungry, Mum,' he replied.

Mr Smith went to the door, paid the driver and came back carrying a huge cardboard box. He always liked to 'go large' when it came to pizzas. A delicious smell wafted from the box. It was so good that even Billy perked up. There was a bit of a delay while they all tried to find the plates, which finally showed up at the bottom of a very deep packing case. Then the family sat down on the floor again and prepared to eat.

Mr Smith opened the cardboard box. **Mmmmmm**, that was such a fine smell! They all hungrily peered inside . . .

. . . AND GOT THE SURPRISE OF THEIR LIVES.

There in the box was a pizza – nothing unusual about that, you might think – but this was a pizza with a rather unusual topping. True, it boasted a generous coating of tomato, a smattering of olives and lashings of cheese, just as you'd expect. But mixed up in all *that* was a shape that looked a little bit . . . furry. A shape that looked considerably *plump* and really quite noticeably *ginger*. In fact, that shape looked EXACTLY like a plump ginger guinea pig. Or, to be more precise, a plump ginger guinea pig who was scoffing a rocket leaf – and looking extremely shifty as he did so.

'HARRY!!!!!!!!' yelled everyone in delight.

'**WHEEK, WHEEEK, WHEEEEK!!!!**' wheeked Harry Stevenson.

Harry Stevenson lay safely snuggled on Billy's lap, nibbling the last of the rocket leaves from the pizza box. Now he wasn't covered in cheese and tomato sauce, Harry could finally relax. It had certainly been a strange day.

Harry looked up into Billy's eyes. They seemed a bit wet for some reason. Harry wished he could talk to Billy. If he could, he'd tell Billy everything – about the dandelions, the cat, the bicycle and the dog.

He'd explain how he'd made one last jump from the dog on to the moped, and wriggled under a pile of pizza boxes as the driver spoke to the teenagers. Then he'd spent five strange hours circling the city as the driver made his deliveries. He'd nearly been spotted a couple of times, but the driver kept going back to the restaurant for new boxes to add to the pile, covering him up again and again.

Harry would tell Billy how he'd given up hope and crept into the very last box to hide. That box had held a lovely surprise – not just pizza but a side salad too. Harry had never heard of 'side salad' before, but he'd certainly enjoyed it!

But Harry couldn't talk the Smiths' language because he was a guinea pig. So instead he had a nibble on the carrot he was offered and fell fast asleep in Billy's arms. Back where he belonged and Billy could only agree. Wherever Harry Stevenson was, that was home.

It felt good to be home.

BOOK 2
Come down,
Harry Stevenson!

CHAPTER 1

Hello again, Harry Stevenson

Harry Stevenson, the greediest guinea pig in the world, woke up from a deep sleep. As usual, the first thing he thought about was food. He combed his whiskers and washed his ginger fur as quickly as possible, then peeped out from his pile of hay. Harry's sparkly eyes darted round the cage. *Phew,*

there was his bowl. It looked nice and full –
no need to worry.

Harry was about to bustle over to the
food bowl when he glanced outside his cage
and got a horrible shock. Everything in the
room – even the windows and door – had
been jumbled up! There was his best friend
Billy Smith's bed, but it was in a different
place to where Harry remembered. The
boxes of building blocks, model dinosaurs
and toy cars had all been moved. Someone
had taken the posters of Sparky FC (Billy's
favourite team) from above his bed and put
them on another wall. And as for the view
out of the window – how had they managed
to change *that*?

For a few moments, Harry stared open-mouthed at the strange scene. Then he remembered. This was Billy and Harry's new bedroom! The Smith family had moved flats a few weeks ago and Harry still wasn't used to the change.

Mystery solved, Harry settled down to breakfast. His bowl had been filled to the top with nuggets, but soon it was empty. Harry Stevenson shook his head sadly. It was a constant problem. There were NEVER enough nuggets in Harry's opinion.

Harry closed his eyes and imagined a big, full bowl piled high with enough nuggets to last the day. What a sight that would be! He gave a little squeak of excitement and jumped into the air, kicking out his legs like a tiny bucking bronco.

As Harry Stevenson popcorned merrily round the cage, Billy came into the room and laughed. Harry skidded to a halt and looked up, pleased. He hadn't heard many laughs from Billy lately. Billy had been very quiet. Harry loved Billy with all his heart and was worried about him.

Billy loved Harry back and always confided in him. As soon as Billy got home from school, he would dump his bag and head straight to Harry. Then they'd curl up together and Billy would tell Harry about his day – all the good bits and the bad bits. Recently, there had been a lot more bad bits than good. Harry knew that his friend was finding things hard after moving house:

just like Harry, Billy hadn't got used to the change.

Harry sighed. Billy had told him that he went to a new school now – his old one was too far away. *Why* Billy had to go to school rather than stay at home, cuddling Harry all day, was something Harry could never understand. He felt very sad when he heard about the new school – Billy said that his classmates were kind, but it just wasn't the same. Billy missed his old friends, and the silly jokes and nicknames they shared. Harry hated to think of his friend being lonely.

There were other things that made Harry worry about Billy. There were simple little things from their old home that never meant much before, but oh, how Billy missed them now. Harry listened as Billy told him all about the trees he used to climb in the park, and the friendly cats he'd passed on the way to his old school. There were the dinner ladies who knew what he liked to eat and what he didn't. And then there was the lady in the newsagent's by the traffic lights, who always gave Billy a friendly wave when he passed. Harry knew that Billy loved that shop and had spent lots of his pocket money there, on sweets and crisps and card collections.

'You understand, don't you, Harry?' asked Billy as he stroked his head. 'Mum and Dad say it will take time and they're right, but I really wish it would hurry up and get easier!'

Harry did the only thing he could to show Billy that everything would be fine – he nuzzled up to his friend and nibbled his fingers.

CHAPTER 2

What's Maya like, Harry Stevenson?

A knock on the door made Billy and Harry look up. Billy's parents, Mr and Mrs Smith, were peering into the room.

'Everything all right, Billy?' said Mrs Smith. 'I hope that guinea pig's behaving himself and not trying his vanishing trick again.'

'We're fine, Mum,' smiled Billy as his parents sat down next to him on the bed.

'Your mum and I have been thinking,' said Mr Smith. 'It's your birthday soon – how about having a party here?'

Harry was surprised! Billy had never had a party at home; he'd always said that the old flat was too small. Maybe there were good things about this new place after all, thought Harry. A party would be just the thing to cheer Billy up. He looked hopefully at his friend – but Billy didn't seem so sure.

'I don't know enough people,' he said.

Mr and Mrs Smith replied that it didn't matter. It would only be a small party, which would help Billy get to know his new friends

better. Besides, there would be more jelly
and ice cream to go round if he didn't invite
lots of people. Harry and Billy thought that
was a *very* good point.

'And you'll ask Maya from next door?' asked Mrs Smith hopefully.

'**NO WAY!!!!**' replied Billy.

Mrs Smith sighed. 'I really don't understand what the problem is,' she said. 'Maya seems like such a nice girl.'

Harry wished he could explain. He knew *exactly* what the problem was.

Harry Stevenson had heard all about Maya Matthews. Oh yes. It had taken a whole load of his finest guinea pig nuzzles and nibbles to calm Billy down when he'd been upset about Maya. In fact, it had taken so many that Harry needed to have a lie-down afterwards. So, as far as Harry was concerned, Maya was bad news. *He* didn't want her at the party either!

Maya and her mum, Mrs Matthews, lived next door. The Smiths didn't know much about Mrs Matthews yet, but Billy said she was kind and always smiled. Harry approved – any friend of Billy's was a friend of his. And, when Harry heard that Mrs Matthews had joined the search party when he'd gone missing on moving day, he liked her even more.

With Maya it was different. Maya was the same age as Billy and went to the same school, but she wasn't friendly at all. Harry knew that Billy had made a real effort with Maya, smiling and saying 'hello' when they passed. But Maya always looked down at the floor, with her long brown hair covering her face. Then she just walked by without replying! In Billy and Harry's opinion, Maya definitely *wasn't* 'such a nice girl'.

'Maybe she's shy,' said Mrs Smith.

'I think she's just rude,' huffed Billy, 'and I don't believe she's got a dog either.'

Maya's dog was a real mystery to the Smith family. *Was* there a dog living next door? They hadn't seen a dog and they hadn't heard one either – not a **BARK**, or a **GROWL**, not even a **WHIMPER**. Billy and Harry had tried to peer in through the Matthews' windows or peep down into their garden, but the so-called dog never appeared. Mrs Matthews explained that something had upset the dog a few weeks ago and he'd stayed in his basket ever since.

'We can't understand it,' she said. 'The poor thing must have had such a shock! He's been like that since the day you moved in.'

Hmm, thought Harry – was that why Maya was so unfriendly? Did she blame Billy for scaring the dog? Billy soon had the same idea. The more he thought about it, the more likely it seemed. And the more likely it seemed, the crosser he felt – and even more of Harry's calming nibbles were needed!

Harry knew that Billy loved all animals. He wished Maya would talk to Billy: she'd realize straight away that Billy would **NEVER** scare her dog. But there was no chance of that now. Billy told Harry he'd stopped trying to be friendly to Maya and looked the other way when she passed. He'd even scowled at her a few times.

'There's no way I'm inviting Maya to the party,' Billy whispered to Harry.

CHAPTER 3

In your hutch,
Harry Stevenson

Billy carefully marked the date of the party on his Sparky FC calendar, and Harry watched him tick off each day as the party got closer. It was on the same day as a huge match between the Sparks and their rivals, Scratchy United

(also known as 'the Scratchies'). Billy had been desperate to go, but the tickets cost a lot of money. Mr Smith said that they could watch it on TV instead, after the party.

Mr Smith loved a party, so he quickly got to work on planning Billy's. Every few days, he'd set off in his scruffy old van and come home with something special for the big event. Harry watched as he proudly showed off a paddling pool, some Sparky FC plastic plates and a huge bag of helium balloons with a can of gas to inflate them. Everything he'd found came from a second-hand shop or a friend's home, which made him even prouder. Then one day there was something for Harry too.

'That guinea pig of yours is getting a bit porky,' said Mr Smith.

Harry looked up from his nugget bowl with a start! He wasn't sure what 'porky' meant – but, from the way Mr Smith was gazing at him, he could tell it wasn't flattering.

'Harry could do with some fresh air and a run around,' said Mr Smith. 'Come and see what I've found!'

Billy and Harry watched from the open window as Mr Smith went out to the van, flung open the back doors and bowed deeply as he revealed what was inside. *Ta–da!!!* It was a beautiful wooden hutch with a wire run.

'There you go, son!' beamed Mr Smith.

'Harry can go outside now. He'll be so happy!'

'Happy' perhaps wasn't the best word to describe Harry Stevenson when he saw that hutch. 'Worried' might be better – or even 'terrified'. Until very recently, Harry had never been outside and in fact had doubted that there really was such a place. It was only on moving day that Harry had left the

old flat – and what an experience *that* had been. Weird things happened outside, thought Harry. It was no place for him!

But poor old Harry didn't have a choice. The Smiths took the hutch into the garden and began to set it up. Harry could hear them talking excitedly. *Hmph!* Harry wished he could talk human too, and then he'd tell the Smiths exactly what he thought about hutches, and fresh air, and outside. But he couldn't, so instead he wriggled into the middle of his pile of hay, huddled down and sulked.

It was no use though. After a while, a big pair of hands scooped Harry Stevenson up and out of the hay. Harry protested noisily.

He squeaked as Mrs Smith carried him through the flat, he squeaked as they went down the garden path and he squeaked as he was placed in the hutch.

'Oh shush, you silly hog,' laughed Mrs Smith.

Harry was *really* miffed now. He gave a very rude **'WHEEK'** and dived under the hay. How DARE his family put him in a hutch – didn't they know that outside was dangerous?

Harry hid in the hay and thought very cross thoughts for quite some time. He ignored Billy when he tried to tempt him out with a dandelion leaf, and even refused to show his face when a slice of melon (his favourite) was offered.

Guinea pigs can be surprisingly stubborn for small, fluffy creatures. But then Harry felt hungry. There was bound to be some food nearby if he dared to look. Just one peep wouldn't hurt, he thought.

He poked his nose out of the hay and sniffed around for danger. The hutch smelled of wood, hay . . . and nuggets. Interesting! Harry stuck his whole head out of the hay and saw his bowl in the corner of the hutch. He checked again for danger (cats, lurking foxes, Mrs Smith laughing at him) then scuttled over to scoff the nuggets.

Crouched down by the bowl, Harry had a good view through the door of the hutch.

He could see the wire run and a vivid green carpet of grass. The Smiths were in the garden, sitting on a picnic rug, having lunch.

Lunch, thought Harry dreamily. What a very fine word that was. *Lunch.* Then all of a sudden his mind jumped from 'lunch' to another word . . .

GRASS!

Oh dear! It was happening again. Poor Harry tried to stop himself, but it was no good. His stomach seemed to be talking directly to his paws. So, although Harry's head was telling them to STOP, his bossy tummy was saying, GO, GO, GO! In fact, it was cheering his paws on! In no time at all, Harry had scampered out of the hutch,

raced three times round the
run and was treating himself to
the best lunch he'd had in ages –
delicious green grass.

'You see, son?' said Mr Smith. 'That's one happy guinea pig.'

And amazingly Mr Smith was right!

Outside isn't so bad after all, thought Harry as he chomped his way round the run. And as for fresh grass . . . **NOM, NOM, NOM!**

CHAPTER 4

Cross your paws,
Harry Stevenson

The day of the party drew nearer and nearer. Harry Stevenson felt very excited. He'd never been to a party before! Harry popcorned happily round the run, bouncing in and out of beams of sunlight. Summer was coming and the weather was getting warm enough to have the party outside.

Billy's mood seemed sunnier too – he'd told his mum and dad that life at school was getting better. He'd got to know some of his classmates and invited them to the party. Mr and Mrs Smith were thrilled that Billy had settled down – but Harry wasn't so sure.

The Smiths got busier and busier. All sorts of making and buying, fetching and carrying were going on. Harry was puzzled – he'd heard that parties were fun but, from what he'd seen so far, they seemed like a lot of work. A party must be something *very* special, Harry thought.

Harry spent most days in the hutch now, only sleeping in his cage in the flat at night. He'd grown to love being outside – basking in the sunshine, nibbling daisies and watching butterflies dance above his head. From the hutch he had a good view of a gap in the fence between the Smiths' and the Matthews' gardens. Harry kept a beady eye on it – looking for signs of the Matthews' mysterious dog – but so far he'd seen nothing. It was very strange.

Now that Harry had an outside hutch as well as an inside cage, he got *two* newspapers to read each week (Billy used them as a sort of carpet for Harry). The sports pages were full of news about Sparky FC – if they managed to beat the Scratchies, they'd win the league!

Harry read every word – he liked to know all about the team so he could share Billy's interest. He'd learned the names of all the players and knew the 'stats' for every game. Harry had even appeared in a match-day programme! Billy had sent in a photo of his friend wearing a Sparky FC bobble hat: seeing that picture printed in the programme was one of the pair's proudest moments. It was now framed on Billy's wall. Harry wished he could have a copy in the hutch too.

In the afternoon, Harry would wait for Billy to come home from school. He'd sit in the doorway of the hutch for hours, peering out hopefully. Then, as soon as he saw Billy in the garden, Harry would **WHEEK** with joy. He'd frolic about in the run while Billy sat and watched him, or, even better, he'd get to curl up on Billy's lap and guzzle dandelions from his friend's hand. Billy would chat and Harry would listen, offering a friendly nuzzle if needed. Those sunny afternoons would have been perfect had Harry not known that Billy was feeling very nervous about the party.

Harry knew that the party meant a lot to Billy – so it meant a lot to him too. A new group of children were coming to their home and Billy didn't know them very well. If the party was fun, it would help him to make friends. But if anything went wrong . . . well, what would the other children think? They might all laugh about it together. Perhaps they'd laugh about Billy!

Harry was worried for Billy. He didn't want him to be laughed at. He wanted a happy Billy. He really hoped Billy would make new friends – the party *had* to go well!

Harry crossed his toes for luck. Everything would be fine, he thought. Worrying never helped. It was only a party, he told himself: what could possibly go wrong?

CHAPTER 5

It's party time, Harry Stevenson

Finally, there were no more dates on the calendar. Today was the day: party time! The Smiths hoped it would be a double celebration, with Sparky FC winning the cup game later in the afternoon. Mr Smith carried the radio around with him so he could listen to the pre-match chat and Billy wore his Sparky FC strip.

Harry Stevenson sat in the doorway of his hutch, chewing contentedly on one carrot after another and watching everyone else work hard. It made Harry tired just to see all the activity – the Smiths buzzed about like mad to get the garden ready, setting up the paddling pool and bringing out games, cushions and rugs to sit on. Billy helped his mum hang streamers and party flags off every fence, tree and bush they could reach.

Meanwhile, Mr Smith spent a very long time blowing up the special balloons. There did seem to be a *lot* of balloons. Every time Mr Smith thought he'd blown the last one up, he reached into the box and pulled out another! So the bunch of balloons grew bigger and bigger and bigger. It needed a very heavy weight to stop it blowing away.

Eventually, Mr Smith reached the last balloon and Mrs Smith ran out of bushes to hang things on. They all stepped back and admired the garden – it was transformed into a party wonderland! Even the washing line was covered with 'Happy Birthday' bunting and the hutch decked out with a Sparky FC flag! The Smiths beamed with pride. But Harry Stevenson felt sleepy after all that work (though he hadn't done any of it himself). He toddled off into the hutch and snuggled into the hay, trying not to worry about the party. He wondered if eating one

or two spinach leaves might help, but it didn't – so he ate twenty. Then he drifted off to sleep.

The party was in full swing by the time Harry woke up. There were four guests: two girls and two boys. Harry had heard all about them from Billy so he had fun trying to guess who was who.

That must be Jake, he thought, looking at a boy with blond hair. Billy had spoken a lot about Jake. *Hmm*, thought Harry, *that means that the dark-haired boy is Daniel.*

As for the girls, Billy had spoken about

a girl with long red hair called Scarlett and a girl with black curly hair called Jess. It wasn't hard to tell them apart! Harry still felt very clever though.

From his spot in the hutch he kept watch over the party like a little guard. Soon everyone was running around happily and making lots of noise. All the children were Sparks fans too, so there was a lot of talk about the match. Harry yawned and stretched. Things were going well – now he could relax.

Mr Smith had thought of all sorts of party games. There was a memory game, and pin the tail on the donkey, and musical chairs (using the cushions Billy had brought outside).

The children had a brilliant time!

I love *parties if they're all like this*, thought Harry Stevenson.

After a while, everyone flopped down on the blankets and relaxed. They all looked up at the clear blue sky, with the big bunch of balloons waving over them.

Then all of a sudden Jake looked at the hutch. 'Can we see your guinea pig?' he asked, and everyone joined in. Harry flushed with pride under his fur! Had Billy been talking about him at school?

'Bring Harry out while we get the tea, Billy,' said Mr Smith as he and Mrs Smith headed off to the kitchen. So Harry got to snuggle up on Billy's lap while everyone admired him. He peered round at the children. Would they make good friends for Billy? They didn't look too bad, he thought, and Billy seemed very happy. Then Billy passed Harry to Jake.

'I know,' said Jake, 'let's wrap him up and play pass the guinea pig!'

They all laughed, apart from Billy. 'Harry wouldn't like that,' he said. 'He might wee on you if he's frightened.'

'Urrrggghhhhhhh!' the others chorused.

Jake turned a funny colour and pulled a face. But then he noticed Billy giving Harry a big cheeky wink.

'BILLY!' cried Jake and everyone laughed.

The party was a huge success so far!

CHAPTER 6

Oh no,
Harry Stevenson

It was time for tea. Harry Stevenson watched with envy as the children filled their plates with sandwiches, pizza, crisps, sausage rolls, tomatoes, grapes and biscuits, and cupcakes iced in the Sparky FC colours. Harry wouldn't have eaten any of those things – but he always liked to see a full plate or bowl!

'Mmmm,' sighed Billy, holding up a slice of pizza. 'My favourite.'

Harry Stevenson disagreed. In his opinion, pizza should be banned. But that wasn't surprising. If you'd been stuck in a cramped box for five hours, going round and round the city on the back of a delivery driver's moped, you'd probably feel the same way!

The children started talking about their favourite foods. Jake liked fish fingers, Daniel's favourite was cheese, Jess loved chicken and Scarlett said that spaghetti was delicious, just the BEST FOOD EVER.

Harry Stevenson pricked up his ears.

Was spaghetti *really* the best food ever? Better than spinach, or carrots, or nuggets? It sounded like something he should try! Harry wasn't too sure what spaghetti looked like, but then the children talked about how it was so hard to catch the long white strands with a fork. Harry listened with interest. Jake said he liked cutting them up into little pieces, while Daniel said he just slurped them up so they made funny noises. Then everyone laughed and agreed that actually spaghetti really *was* the best food ever.

Harry was thrilled to see everyone having such a good time, and felt so relaxed that he started to doze off. He lazed on the blanket, surrounded by sandwiches and crisps. As he drifted off to sleep, he heard the children talking about him.

'Ahh!' they cooed. 'He looks so cute.'

'It looks like he's dreaming about food,' said Billy. 'I think he always does – it's his favourite thing.'

Billy was right. Harry was having a lovely dream about food. Or, to be more precise, Harry was dreaming about 'the best food ever'. In Harry's dream, spaghetti grew in the garden and he could nibble it like grass. It was delicious! The children giggled as Harry smacked his lips in his sleep. Then Jess threw a crisp at Billy, and Billy tickled Jake, and soon everyone forgot about Harry as they chased each other round the garden.

Oblivious to the noise, Harry slept on, chomping on imaginary dream spaghetti. It really was extremely tasty. But, as Harry dreamed, the spaghetti started to get chewier. Soon he needed to bite really hard. Then another strange thing happened: in his dream, Harry to started to float! Flying while scoffing spaghetti wasn't a bad feeling at all. It was, well . . . dreamy. As Harry floated along, he heard voices calling from far away. They were very faint at first, but got louder, and louder, and louder . . .

'HARRY!!!!'

Harry Stevenson woke up to find he was dangling in the air! It hadn't been spaghetti he'd been nibbling in his dream – he had a real-life mouthful of balloon strings! Harry's eyes opened wide with surprise. His teeth had cut some of the strings, and the remaining ones were not strong enough to tie the enormous bunch of balloons down. They were snapping one by one. **PING, PING, PING!** As each string snapped, the balloons (and Harry) rose up a bit more.

Well, thought Harry as he drifted above the picnic blanket, *this is unexpected!* He was too surprised to be scared and just held on tight with his teeth.

'HARRY!' yelled Billy,
sending paper plates, cushions
and uneaten sandwiches flying as he ran to
catch his airborne friend. But, just as Billy
reached the blanket, a gust of wind snapped
the remaining strings. The balloons were
now floating free. They flew across the
garden, taking Harry with them.

'HARRY!' cried the children as they
chased the bunch of balloons through the
flower beds. From the outside it looked like
a party game, and indeed 'Catch the flying
guinea pig' would have made an excellent
game – if every second the balloons hadn't
been rising a tiny bit higher, and Harry
looked more and more worried.

Suddenly, a really big gust of wind blew through the garden.

WHOOSH! Up went the balloons and up went Harry!

CHAPTER 7

Up, up, up, Harry Stevenson

'Come down, Harry Stevenson, come down!' cried the children, but Harry couldn't let go now – he was too high up!

Harry looked back and wished he hadn't. He could see the children running around, jumping up with their arms outstretched in vain to grab him. He could see the chaos of the garden as the picnic was kicked everywhere. And there were Mr and Mrs Smith, standing motionless on the garden path, looking up, open-mouthed with surprise. Mrs Smith was clutching Billy's birthday cake, its eight candles flickering forlornly in the breeze.

There was another gust of wind, much stronger this time, and the balloons soared upwards. The children in the garden grew smaller and smaller below Harry Stevenson. Soon he could see the roof of the flats. The wind was blowing him away from the block now.

The calls of the children grew fainter, until they died away in the

distance. But now Harry could hear deeper, older voices crying out in surprise. The spectacle of a flying guinea pig was causing quite a stir on the streets below.

Harry watched as one lady walked straight into a lamp post as she stared up at the sky. **OUCH!** That looked painful. Several people stood frozen in amazement, dropping their shopping bags on to the ground as Harry and the balloons sailed overhead. One poor man's shopping fell all over the road and rolled down a hill, but the man didn't notice because he was too busy looking up.

It would have been funny if Harry hadn't been in such a pickle himself.

But soon those voices faded too. Up, up, up flew Harry Stevenson, into the silent sky. The traffic noises and the hubbub of the city faded away as he passed through chilly, damp clouds.

Harry couldn't hold on with his teeth much longer. Luckily, the longer strings had tangled themselves round his body, forming a kind of sling that supported him. Now he was quite safe – well, as safe as a guinea pig could be when floating through the clouds and supported only by balloons.

Harry mostly kept his eyes tightly shut, but every now and again he dared to look

down. Just how much bigger could 'outside' get, he wondered? It just went on and on and on – and then it went on some more!

If Harry had been able to enjoy it, the city below made a wonderful view for a guinea pig who didn't get out much. He couldn't spot the flats now, they were too far away, but he could see the grid-like pattern of the city streets, the green splodges of the parks, and tower blocks that looked like little cardboard boxes. Harry couldn't believe how many homes there were and how many people must live in them. He wondered if there were lots of guinea pigs below him too.

Up ahead, Harry could see some dots in the sky. They were quite far away, but they were moving very fast towards him. As the dots got nearer, they turned into bird shapes. It was a huge flock of seagulls! The gulls got nearer and nearer until it looked like the whole crowd would crash into the balloons and send Harry tumbling to the ground.

Harry gulped. He'd never liked birds – they kept him awake with their pesky singing and now they were going to be the end of him!

Those birds don't look very friendly, thought Harry.

As they got closer, he saw sharp, pointy

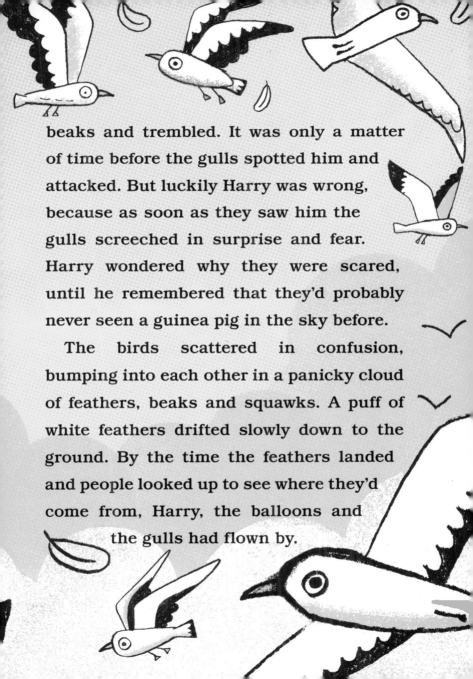

beaks and trembled. It was only a matter of time before the gulls spotted him and attacked. But luckily Harry was wrong, because as soon as they saw him the gulls screeched in surprise and fear. Harry wondered why they were scared, until he remembered that they'd probably never seen a guinea pig in the sky before.

The birds scattered in confusion, bumping into each other in a panicky cloud of feathers, beaks and squawks. A puff of white feathers drifted slowly down to the ground. By the time the feathers landed and people looked up to see where they'd come from, Harry, the balloons and the gulls had flown by.

CHAPTER 8

Look out, Harry Stevenson!

'Follow that guinea pig!' yelled Mr Smith as he drove the van at top speed down the street. They had jumped in as soon as they'd seen Harry fly off. Tyres screeched, rubber burned and the exhaust popped loudly as the poor old van charged along. It really wasn't built for speed, even when new – and that had been a long, long time ago.

Mr Smith needed to keep his eyes on the road, so Mrs Smith kept track of Harry. She leaned out of the passenger side window, twisting round to look up, trying to spot the balloons as they raced across the sky.

'Go left!' she'd cry or, 'Quick, go right!'

Billy and his friends were on the back seats of the van, peering over the front seats and trying to see out too. Billy felt numb with shock. Poor, poor Harry! Would he ever see his best friend again? And then he thought of what people at school would say: how the others would talk about his disastrous birthday party and his dad's stupid, scruffy old van.

Everyone will laugh, thought Billy, who was trying not to cry. *This was going to be such a brilliant day, with the party and the football – but now it's all gone wrong and Harry's lost forever!*

But suddenly he felt Jake patting his

arm. He turned round to see a friendly face looking at him.

'It'll be OK,' said Jake. 'Don't worry. Harry looks like he can handle anything – even flying.'

Billy gave a small smile. 'It's the landing I'm worried about,' he said. 'But thanks, Jake.'

Up in the air, Harry Stevenson was starting to worry about landing too. A couple of the balloons had gone **POP**, and the bunch was slowly starting to sink. Soon quite a few more balloons had popped. Each time, Harry and the remaining balloons plunged down quickly. It was like a horrible fairground ride – the sort that makes your tummy feel like it's turning upside-down. Harry held on grimly with his teeth and wrapped himself up more tightly in the strings.

The balloons continued to float down. Buildings, roads and trees below got bigger and bigger again. It was like zooming in on the city with a microscope. As Harry got lower, he left the eerie quiet of the sky and sounds started to come back. Harry heard cars honking, dogs barking and a strange roaring noise that he couldn't identify.

Harry looked ahead – *oh no!* He was

heading directly for a big, tall building. It was HUGE and had such an unusual shape that Harry had no idea what it was for. The only thing he could tell for sure was that it *definitely* wouldn't be a soft landing.

The balloons were coming down fast now. The roaring noise got louder as Harry

whizzed towards the building. It took all his nerve to hold on tight and not open his mouth to **WHEEEK** in panic.

Perhaps this is what the end of the world sounds like? thought Harry as the roaring filled his ears. He braced himself for a very nasty bump, but, just as it seemed he would

fly smack into a wall, a gust of wind flung him up again and he continued his rollercoaster ride, up to the top of the building and over its roof.

Phew! thought Harry – until the wind died down, the balloons plummeted and he saw the ground whizzing up towards him . . .

YIKES! thought Harry Stevenson, readying himself for the crash. There was a flash of green, a mighty roar, a squeak and a bump as Harry hit the ground.

CHAPTER 9

They think it's all over, Harry Stevenson

Harry Stevenson lay winded for a few moments. The balloons had floated off when their strings snapped in the fall. Luckily, Harry's plump, round tummy saved him from injury. He still felt strange though: his sight was so blurry that all he could see was green, and his ears were filled with that weird roaring noise.

Gradually, Harry's sight focused and he realized where he was. The green he'd seen was grass. But it wasn't any old grass – oh no. It was the grass of a football pitch: a great big massive football pitch, inside a great big massive stadium. And the roaring noise wasn't in his head or the sound of the end of the world. It was the voice of a football crowd.

Harry Stevenson had landed slap-bang in the middle of the Sparky FC v. Scratchy United match!!

If you've ever been inside a football stadium, you'll know just how big they are. But now imagine that you're about twelve centimetres tall – and that's on a good day, with your head held high. Harry Stevenson definitely *wasn't* having a good day. To Harry, the sides of the stadium looked as high as the mountains that he had seen in Billy's magazines. They towered up to the sky, filled with thousands and thousands of people, all singing and shouting and chanting. The noise was deafening.

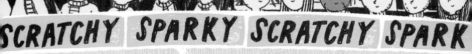

SCRATCHY SPARKY SCRATCHY SPARK

Harry wondered why nobody seemed to have noticed him. But then he saw the Scratchy United team celebrating at the other end of the pitch. The enormous roar he'd heard on landing was for the Scratchies scoring a penalty. Every eye in the stadium had been focused on that goal. Harry glanced up at the scoreboard. It was 1–1, with only minutes of the match left to play.

Harry peered around and decided to head for safety at the edge of the pitch. He scuttled across the grass as quickly as his little legs could carry him. But, before he could get far, Harry saw with horror that the ball, and the footballers, were heading straight for him!

'**WHEEK!!**' said Harry Stevenson, racing across the pitch. But oh, that pitch was huge and Harry was only small. It was too late to run – there was no escape! Through his paws, Harry could feel the earth shake as the players thundered towards him. He was going to be trampled!

'**WHEEEK!**' shrilled Harry as the ball bounced just a whisker's length in front of him. He jumped high into the air to avoid it, but instead he landed on the ball! As it rolled along, Harry had to scamper like a hamster in a wheel to stay on top. If he fell off, or the players caught up, Harry would be squashed by about twenty ginormous football boots. Harry had seen Billy's boots – those studs looked painful. So he ran and ran.

Poor Harry was so scared that his little legs moved in a blur as he scurried this way and that to escape the footballers.

Steered by Harry, the ball sped across the pitch in crazy loops and patterns, with the players chasing close behind. They went up and down the field and round and round in circles – but the teams were too focused

on winning the match to notice anything unusual.

Then a voice from the crowd called: 'Look! There's a **GUINEA PIG** on the ball!'

For a moment, there was pure silence around the stadium. The players stopped dead in their tracks. Then the whole crowd gasped out loud! The people in the rows nearest Harry stood up to get a better look, then the rows behind them did too, and before long the entire stadium was doing a Mexican wave as everyone tried to get a good view of Harry. Fifty thousand camera phones flashed and the commentators jabbered excitedly. They'd never seen anything like it!

Harry was still running on the ball,

heading for a gap in the hoardings by the side of the pitch. But now ALL the players chased after the ball to catch him. Harry dived and dodged between them. He was amazingly speedy and nimble! Then he saw a huge, scary-looking Scratchy United player run in front of him, arms outstretched.

'**WHEEEEEEEKKKKK!**' wheeked Harry, running on the ball like mad. He ducked left, he sped right and he steered the ball straight through the player's legs. **POW!** The ball hit the net and Harry was thrown into the air. Luckily, the net broke his fall and he landed with a thump on the ground. What was a safety net doing on a football pitch, wondered Harry in confusion? Then he realized that it was the back of a goal . . . and the Sparky FC players seemed to be celebrating!

'*GOOOALLLLLLL!*' screamed the Sparky FC crowd.

'HUH?' gasped the Scratchy United team in disbelief.

PEEEEPPP! blasted the referee's whistle. The match was over!

CHAPTER 10

Nice one,
Harry Stevenson

Every TV and radio station in the land switched to the Sparky FC ground, where the stadium was in uproar.

'Quite extraordinary scenes are taking place here at the Sparky-Scratchy match!' yelled the commentators. 'Footballing history is literally being made! We've just seen the first-ever goal by a guinea pig – *surely* it can't be allowed?'

The poor referee was in the middle of a huddle of players, scratching his head and consulting the football rulebook. It was a very big book indeed. After a while, he slammed it shut and blew his whistle for silence. There was nothing in the rules to say that a guinea pig *couldn't* score a goal, he said, and anyway the last player to kick the ball had been the Sparky captain – so the goal could stand!

The final score was 2–1 to Sparky FC – the Sparks had won the league!

The stadium erupted in joy and even the Scratchy supporters saw the funny side.

It was certainly an unforgettable match! Harry was lifted up by the Sparky team like a furry trophy and paraded around the ground. Scores of photographers ran on to the pitch, and Harry was jostled this way and that as they all tried to get the best

photo. Soon they started shouting at each other. Harry was passed from person to person, people tried to grab him and bright lights flashed in his face. He was terrified.

Suddenly, he heard a high, clear voice over the noise of the stadium. The voice sounded familiar, but Harry couldn't place it.

'STOP!! Leave that guinea pig alone NOW!'

Harry looked up. There, elbowing cameras out of the way as she marched into the scrum to rescue him, was a dark-haired girl dressed from head to toe in the Sparky FC kit.

It was Maya Matthews!

'It's all right, Harry,' whispered Maya, taking him gently in her arms. 'I'll look after you.'

Peering up gratefully, Harry saw only kindness in Maya's face. He was surprised at how calm and safe he felt with her. Oh dear, he thought – had he and Billy been wrong to think badly of Maya? And it looked like she was a massive Sparky fan too!

But before he could think any more, Harry heard a car horn honking, a screech of tyres and more cheers from the crowds. For there was the Smiths' van speeding into view, backfiring madly and skidding to a halt in the middle of the pitch!

The van doors opened and everyone

jumped out, then ran over to Maya and Harry.

'MAYA!! You've got him!' yelled Billy, so happy that he forgot he wasn't talking to her.

Maya flushed bright red and put her head down, so her long brown hair was covering her face. But Harry had a good view from below and could see that she was smiling. *Aha*, he thought, *she's shy after all. Mrs Smith was right!*

Then Maya looked Billy in the eye and smiled.

'That's OK,' she said.

And she passed Harry Stevenson over to Billy, who held him up and kissed him again

and again. Harry snuggled up to Billy's face.
It felt so good to be back with his best friend.

Harry Stevenson looked out from the safety of Billy's arms, taking in the sights and sounds of the stadium. Everything felt better now he was with his friend again. Harry was just about to relax when he saw a police officer and her dog striding over to them.

Oh no, he thought, *Mr Smith shouldn't have driven on to the pitch – he's going to be arrested!* He watched helplessly as the police officer got closer . . .

'Hi, Mum!' called Maya. 'Hi, Mack!'

Seeing that everyone was staring in

amazement, Maya started to explain. 'Mum's on duty today. I always come along when she's working here. And it's Mack's first day back at work as a police dog. He's not been feeling great lately, but he's better now – aren't you, boy?'

Harry stared in surprise. Maya really *did* have a dog – and it looked familiar. It was a big, shaggy-looking dog. Its teeth looked quite big too. Harry tried to remember – now where had he seen that shaggy fur before?

Oh dear. It was the dog he'd ridden on moving day! And not just ridden – he'd bitten Mack as well! Harry Stevenson gulped and waited to be bitten back.

But Mack was also staring in horror. As soon as he'd sniffed Harry, he remembered the horrible, scary dash across the park. He started trembling, his tail between his legs.

'Mack, you silly doggy,' scolded Maya. 'Look, it's only a guinea pig. He's tiny! He can't possibly hurt you!'

Mack looked at Harry again. He could see that a small, fluffy creature like Harry couldn't do much harm. Maybe he'd been mistaken. It must have been something else that had been so scary in the park – something that smelled the same, but was much, much fiercer.

So Mack leaned forward and licked Harry on the face.

Phew, thought Harry, who opened his eyes and licked Mack back.

Maya clapped her hands with delight.

'You two are going to be friends, I know it,' she said.

Mack and Harry weren't the only ones who were going to be good friends. It looked like the drama of Harry's rescue was going to be the start of some firm friendships for Billy. Back in the Smiths' garden, Harry listened as the children talked nineteen to the dozen about the amazing day they'd had. He was happily snuggled in a nest that Billy had made for him from Sparky FC scarves. The

Matthews family had come round too – Mrs Matthews helped Mr and Mrs Smith tidy up the garden and Mack curled up next to Maya, wagging his tail every now and again.

'This is the best party ever!' said Scarlett. 'I can't believe we met the team!'

Sparky FC had the won the league because of Harry, so he and his friends had been asked to take part in the trophy ceremony. They'd walked proudly up the steps with the team, where a huge golden trophy and silver medals for the players were awarded. There were even some spare medals for the children – and Harry, of course. As the Sparky FC captain held up the trophy to the crowd, Billy had held up Harry!

'HA-REE, HA-REE!' chanted the crowd. 'There's only one Harry Stevenson, one Harry Steeeevenson!'

Harry Stevenson snuggled further into his nest of scarves and yawned. What a day! He tried to nibble on his medal, but spat it out – *UGH!* He wished everyone had been given a nice bunch of carrots instead.

Mr Smith went out to the van to look for Billy's cake. It took a while to find because it had landed on the floor of the van during the mad dash through the city, and then it had slid under a seat. It was a bit squashed – but it would do.

Billy blew the candles out while everyone sang 'Happy Birthday'. Mack barked along and even Harry Stevenson gave a few cheery burbles. Then everyone tucked in, eating every last crumb. It tasted delicious, even the dusty bits.

And then it was time for the guests to go home.

'Thanks, Billy,' said Jake, Daniel, Scarlett, Jess and Maya as they left. 'That was **BRILLIANT!** We'll see you at school!'

That evening, all the Smiths (and Harry) sat on Billy's bed as he opened his presents. They were mostly to do with Sparky FC – perfect! Billy sighed with happiness.

His birthday hadn't turned out *quite* as he'd expected, but it had ended in the best possible way. He was even looking forward to school next week – and it was all thanks to Harry Stevenson.

Mr and Mrs Smith smiled to see Billy looking so content.

'What d'you fancy for dinner, Billy?' asked Mrs Smith. 'Spaghetti?'

There was a mad furry scramble and a piercing **WHHHEEEEEK!** as Harry Stevenson dived for cover.

'Blimey,' said Mr Smith. 'What's upset Harry?!'

One thing Harry knew for certain was that he was NEVER eating spaghetti again!

THE END

DID YOU KNOW?

Harry Stevenson loves being Billy's best friend, but in real life Harry would be very sad if he were the only guinea pig in the family. Just like us, guinea pigs are happiest being with a friend or in a family group, so if you're thinking of inviting a guinea pig into your own home, ask him or her to bring a friend! That way you'll have the chattiest, perkiest pets possible.

Ali Pye has drawn Harry's cage smaller than it should be, so it fits on to the pages in this book. Harry said he didn't mind, so long as we pointed out that guinea pigs need a really decent-sized cage to scamper about in. Your family can find lots of information online about the right sort of cage, bedding and diet needed to keep your guinea pig friends popcorning with happiness.

Guinea pigs are not pigs and they don't come from Guinea! They originated in the Andes – a range of mountains in South America. Harry Stevenson has seen the Andes in a nature programme he watched with Billy. He wasn't very impressed, though, because they looked extremely chilly and there didn't seem to be any nuggets there.

The other name for a guinea pig is 'cavy' which is the short version of their official name: Cavia Porcellus. A female guinea pig is called a 'sow' and the males are referred to as 'boars'. Harry Stevenson was a bit touchy about this, until Billy explained that, 'No, Harry, it doesn't mean you are boring'.

Harry is very proud of his family tree. He claims that his great-great-great-great-great-great-great-great-great-great-great-grandma was painted for a famous portrait! Despite a lot of checking we can't confirm this – but it's certainly true that a guinea pig really is shown in a painting from 1580, together with a little girl and her brothers. The painting is now in the National Portrait Gallery in London.

Guinea pigs like Harry make the most amazing pets, but they need careful looking after. If you are thinking of owning guinea pigs, make sure you do all the reading you can about how to make sure they are safe, well and happy. Have a look at pet rescues too – there are lots of beautiful, friendly piggies out there needing new homes. And, by the way, once you have guinea pigs, it's probably best to keep your new friends away from bicycle baskets, pizza boxes, balloons and spaghetti!!

DID YOU SPOT?

Book 1

WHO chased Harry along the wall?
Can you remember his name?

WHAT was the colour of the coat worn
by Mack's owner in the park?

WHY does Harry end up in a pizza box?
How did he manage that?!

Book 2

WHAT are some of the things that Billy
misses from living in the Smiths' old flat?

WHO comes to Billy's birthday party?
(There are four names to remember.)

WHY was it so important for Sparky FC to
win the football match – and what was the
name of the team they played?

Answers:
Book 1: Mr Snuggles; Pink; He jumped on to a
pizza delivery moped and hid in one of the pizza boxes!
Book 2: His friends, the trees in the park, friendly cats, dinner ladies
and the newsagent; Jake, Daniel, Scarlet and Jess; Sparky FC played
Scratchy United ("the Scratchies") in the League final!

HARRY WORD SEARCH!

Can you find these five words from the book?

BALLOONS BILLY HARRY PIZZA SPARKY FC

B	X	F	X	O	K	W	U	S	M
A	Y	E	G	O	X	E	P	P	Y
L	B	I	L	L	Y	N	V	A	W
L	V	Y	Z	H	R	V	S	R	C
O	L	V	P	T	A	J	H	K	P
O	M	H	Y	V	X	T	P	Y	K
N	G	L	A	O	V	K	I	F	H
S	C	H	L	R	U	O	Z	C	Z
V	Y	I	V	K	R	S	Z	L	F
F	X	M	R	M	L	Y	A	A	Q

Ali Pye is the author and illustrator of
The Adventures of Harry Stevenson.
The book was inspired by a real-life
guinea pig (who turned out to be a girl
and was re-named Harriet Stevenson).
She lives in Twickenham with
her husband, children and two
guinea pigs: Beryl and Badger.

LOOK OUT FOR MORE HARRY STEVENSON ADVENTURES COMING SOON!